Part-Time Dog

by Jane Thayer

pictures by Lisa McCue

HarperCollinsPublishers

To Gabriel and Emma, with my love
—J.T.

For CappuChewie, Kapusta, Whisky, Cooper, Simba, Maggie,
Doppler, Dexter, Toby, Rory, Beauregard, Isabella, Mitzi,
and my very own full-time dog, Labradoodle Dundee
—L.M.

Part-Time Dog • Text copyright © 1954, 2004 by Catherine Woolley • Illustrations copyright © 2004 by Lisa McCue • Manufactured in
China by South China Printing Company Ltd. All rights reserved. • www.harperchildrens.com • Library of Congress Cataloging-in-Publication Data
Thayer, Jane. • Part-time dog / by Jane Thayer ; pictures by Lisa McCue • p. cm. • Summary: A homeless little dog finds supper at one house, a comfortable
couch at a second, and breakfast at a third. ISBN 0-06-029693-3 — ISBN 0-06-029692-5 (lib. bdg.) 1. Dogs—Juvenile fiction. [1. Dogs—Fiction.
2. Neighbors—Fiction.] I. McCue, Lisa, ill. II. Title. • PZ10.3.T2785 Par 2004 • 00-050561 • [E]—dc21 • This story was first published in 1954
in *Humpty Dumpty's Magazine for Little Children*. • A hardcover edition of this book was published in 1965 by William Morrow & Company.
Typography by Rachel Schoenberg 1 2 3 4 5 6 7 8 9 10 ❖ First Edition

A little brown dog with a wagging tail appeared on Maple Street one day.
"Hello, Brownie," the children said, patting his head.

Brownie trotted to school with them.

"Go home," said the teacher.

Where was home?

Brownie trotted back to Maple Street.

Mrs. Atkins was sweeping her walk.
Brownie hurried to help her.
"Go home," Mrs. Atkins said kindly.

Brownie went to the bank with Mrs. Butterworth.
"Go home," she said politely.

He galloped to help Mrs. Tweedy rake her yard.
"Go home," she said politely and kindly.

Brownie liked Maple Street.
People were kind to him.
When the children came home,
he chased a ball until his pink
tongue lolled out.

But then the children went in to dinner
and shut their doors.
Brownie had no place to go.

He sniffed a garbage can for a bone or anything to eat.

Nobody was his friend tonight because everyone thought he was somebody else's dog.

He slept under a porch, but he was cold and hungry and lonely.

In the morning Brownie was shivering, and his poor little stomach was empty. But he smelled a wonderful smell, and he ran to the door where the smell was coming from.

"Woof."

Mrs. Atkins looked out. "Are you hungry?"

"Woof!"

She gave him a beef bone she had meant to make into soup.

Brownie gobbled every bit.

The bone was delicious.

That night Brownie wasn't so hungry. But he was cold.
He trotted to another door.
"Why don't you go home?" asked Mrs. Butterworth.
She looked out.
"Oh, it's snowing! Would you like to sleep in my kitchen?"
"Woof!"
Mrs. Butterworth shut the living-room door to keep
Brownie off her best blue sofa. "Good night."
But the kitchen floor was hard.
So after a while Brownie pushed the door open and
happily fell asleep on Mrs. Butterworth's best blue sofa.

The next morning Mrs. Butterworth cried,
"Get off my sofa!"
Brownie politely said good-bye —"Woof!"—and
left without waiting for breakfast.

He smelled coffee at another house
and trotted over. "Woof!"
"Just in time for breakfast," Mrs.
Tweedy told him.
She gave him a cup of coffee with
cream and sugar and a piece of
buttered toast to crunch.

Brownie was warm and full of buttered toast.
He frisked to school with the Maple Street children.

That night he woofed at Mrs. Atkins's door, and she fed him some leftover lamb she had meant to make into stew.

Then Brownie trotted to Mrs. Butterworth's, forgetting about her best blue sofa.

Mrs. Butterworth saw the snow.

She looked into Brownie's trusting eyes.

She covered her best blue sofa with an old blanket for Brownie.

In the mornings Brownie had coffee and toast with Mrs. Tweedy. And Mrs. Atkins gave him dinner every night until finally she told him, "You are expensive to feed! I don't want a dog! Let's see if Mrs. Butterworth knows whose dog you are."

Brownie thought he was Maple Street's dog, but he was delighted to visit his friend Mrs. Butterworth.

"He sleeps on my best blue sofa," said Mrs. Butterworth. "But I don't know whose dog he is. I don't want a dog. Dogs leave hair on everything! Let's ask Mrs. Tweedy."

"I give him toast and coffee," Mrs. Tweedy told them. "But I don't want a dog. I like to travel, and a dog would tie me down."

They all looked at Brownie, who looked back trustingly.

"He has no license," said Mrs. Atkins.

"He runs around loose," Mrs. Butterworth added.

"We should call the dogcatcher!" Mrs. Tweedy decided.

Brownie wagged his tail.

"I don't want to call the dogcatcher!" Mrs. Tweedy cried.

"He's such a nice dog," Mrs. Atkins moaned.

"I suppose I have to," said Mrs. Butterworth.

Brownie stopped wagging his tail because
Mrs. Butterworth was unhappy.

The dogcatcher came.
Brownie wagged his tail trustingly.

Off Brownie went in the truck.

That night Mrs. Atkins cooked a pork chop for her dinner, but she couldn't eat.

Next door Mrs. Butterworth couldn't sleep.

And the next morning Mrs. Tweedy didn't enjoy her toast and coffee.

"He trusted us," she said. "How could we be so mean?"

She grabbed her bag and out she went.

She met Mrs. Atkins and Mrs. Butterworth with their bags. "I'm going to buy a license for Brownie and get him back!" Mrs. Tweedy cried. "Even if he does tie me down."

"I was going to get him back!" Mrs. Atkins cried. "Even if he is expensive to feed!"

"I was going to get him!" Mrs. Butterworth exclaimed. "Even if he does leave dog hair on my sofa. We can't be mean to someone who trusts us."

Now they all wanted Brownie.

Finally, Mrs. Tweedy had an idea. "We can put a fence around our three backyards so he can play there. I'll feed him breakfast," she said. "I love to see him lap up coffee with sugar and cream and crunch buttered toast."

Mrs. Butterworth said, "He can sleep on my blue sofa. I don't mind a few brown hairs."

"I always have bones to spare," Mrs. Atkins assured them.

"That's breakfast, dinner, and bed. He belongs to all of us! He's our part-time dog!"

"Let's go get him!" Mrs. Tweedy cried.
They climbed into Mrs. Butterworth's
car and rushed to the dogcatcher's . . .

. . . where Brownie waited trustingly.

Then Brownie sat in the front seat,
delighted to be a part-time dog, as
they all drove off to buy his license.